Contents

ROSE'S HOUSE

POPPY'S HOUSE

BUNNY NURSERY

OAKWINGS ACADEMY

BLOSSOM WOOD

WHISPERING WATERFALL

NINAD'S HOUSE

THE WISE WILLOW TREE

SUNSHINE BEACH

Chapter One

The sun shone brightly as Poppy
Merrymoss and her best friends Rose
and Ninad watched the beautiful
yellow-spotted butterfly landing on
their teacher's arm.

"It's beautiful!" Poppy breathed as
the butterfly took off again. Its flapping
wings wafted a gentle breeze over
Poppy's face. The class all grinned as it

flew over their heads.

They were having their lesson out in the gardens of Oakwings Academy, the huge ancient oak tree in the middle of the forest.

"Whenever any animals need our help, they come here to our animal sanctuary," Dr Littlewing told them, pointing to a willow shed nestled among the roots of the academy. She was a tall fairy, with long, flowing black hair that almost reached the floor. Animal-mad Ninad already had his nose pressed to the window of the shed. Poppy peeked in too. All along the sides there were rows of little pens with all kinds of creatures inside. "It is our job as fairies to help the animals and creatures however we can."

They followed their teacher through the sanctuary. It was even nicer on the inside. It smelled of hay and straw and the honey cough syrup Poppy's mum had always given her when she was sick. And there were so many animals!

"Oh look!" Rose shouted. Her wings buzzed excitedly as they passed a small, fluffy grey bunny with a bandaged paw.

"What happened to these mice, Dr Littlewing?" Poppy asked, peering into a cosy pen filled with soft straw. A family of mice slept soundly inside, snuggled up together.

"Their home was destroyed by a storm," Dr Littlewing explained. "They are staying here until we can build them a new home."

The students gathered around as she

held up her wand. "Time to learn a spell," she called. She pointed over to the sanctuary doors and they opened wide.

"Hold out your wands," she instructed, "and wave them like this."

She moved her wand slowly from side to side, creating a breeze.

Poppy copied the movement with her own oak wand.

"We are going to call to the butterflies," Dr Littlewing continued. "Now very quietly, hum a lovely, simple tune. It doesn't matter what the tune is, just imagine the butterflies dancing in the air as you hum."

Poppy concentrated hard. She waved her wand and hummed a tune that her mum always sang to help her baby sister, Daisy, fall asleep. Suddenly,

hundreds of butterflies of all colours
and sizes streamed through the door.
They danced around the fairies. One
flew close to Poppy's face and tickled
her nose.

She giggled. "What do we do now?" she asked.

"We need to move the butterflies into a pen so that I can give them some medicine to protect them against butterfly pox," Dr Littlewing explained.

She ushered a couple of butterflies into a net-covered pen.

Rose excitedly flew at a group of butterflies, but instead of them moving towards the pen, they scattered in all directions.

"Slowly, Rose," Dr Littlewing said.

Poppy joined the other fairies, quietly humming as she led the butterflies

14

into the pen. Soon they were all safely inside.

Dr Littlewing held out a leaf with a drop of gooey-looking golden liquid on it to the yellow-spotted butterfly. The butterfly unfurled its long tongue and drank it up.

"She sucks the medicine through her proboscis – that's her tongue," Dr Littlewing explained. "There is a leaf with medicine for each of you. Use the butterfly spell again to call them to you and make sure they drink it all up."

Poppy held out her wand and hummed. In no time, a small, light blue butterfly landed on her arm.

"It worked!" she cried out as the little butterfly poked out its tongue to drink the medicine.

Beside her, Rose had managed to call a butterfly as well, but this one was twice the size of Poppy's and instead of landing on Rose's arm, it

perched on her head.

Rose burst into nervous giggles. "It tickles!" she laughed.

Ninad was having better luck. His arms were covered in butterflies. He carefully fed them their medicine one by one.

"You're a natural, Ninad," Dr Littlewing said.

Ninad beamed. "I want to be an animal fairy," he said. "But my parents are both water fairies." His grin faded. "I have a willow wand just like them."

"Well, *I'm* an animal fairy," Dr Littlewing said. "But I have a bamboo wand like most air fairies. Don't give up on your dream."

Ninad's eyes lit up. "Maybe I *could* become an animal fairy!"

A loud scream pierced the quiet, sending butterflies swirling around the pen. Dr Littlewing rushed over to Celeste, Poppy and Rose's roommate.

"It keeps trying to stick its tongue in my ear!" she shrieked.

Rose giggled. "I think it thinks you are a flower, Celeste!"

"You do kind of look like a flower," Poppy said. Celeste was wearing a yellow petal dress with curled green

leaves on the sleeves.

Celeste glared at them both.

"Uh oh, we're in trouble with Celeste
– again!" Rose joked. She hooked her
arm in Poppy's. "I'm so glad that you're
my roommate too."

Dr Littlewing shut the rest of the
butterflies in the pen and continued the
lesson. "Now, before the butterflies get
their wings, they're a different type of
creature . . ."

"Caterpillars!" Ninad cried, looking
at the pen full of wriggly green
creatures.

"We are going to learn a spell to help

these caterpillars into their cocoons,"
Dr Littlewing said. "They are ready
to begin their journey to becoming
butterflies."

She knelt beside a caterpillar and
stroked its head. Then she slowly
moved her wand in a circle motion
in front of the caterpillar's eyes. The
caterpillar watched the wand go
around and around. Slowly its eyelids
started to droop and a silky cocoon
began to wind around and around the
caterpillar. Starting from the bottom,
it wound all the way up until the
caterpillar was completely covered in

the silky sleeping bag.

"Now you try," Dr Littlewing said.

Poppy sat beside a furry green caterpillar and stroked its head. It felt soft and a bit spiky. She twirled her wand around, watching as the cocoon worked its way up until her caterpillar was safely snug inside.

"Are these caterpillar eggs?" Ninad called to Dr Littlewing, pointing at a cluster of speckled white eggs in the corner of the pen.

"I think so," Dr Littlewing said excitedly. "But they have markings that I've never seen before. I'm not sure what type of butterflies they will be."

"That one's moving!" Ninad said, pointing to an enormous cocoon hanging at the back of the next pen.

"It's going to hatch." Dr Littlewing smiled.

The fairies gathered around as Dr Littlewing stroked the cocoon. "You're

almost there," she whispered. "Just a little more."

Poppy gasped as two spindly legs appeared from the cocoon, and a blue butterfly emerged. It was huge — twice as big as Dr Littlewing!

"It's a Ulysses butterfly," Dr Littlewing said. "Some fairies ride on them for long journeys."

It sat on top of the cocoon, unfurling its giant wings and moving them slowly back and forth to dry them out.

It was having trouble moving one of its wings, so Dr Littlewing held out her wand and did a small spell. There was a

flash of glittery
light and the
butterfly's
wing moved
freely.

Dr Littlewing
sighed.

"What's wrong?"
Poppy asked. "Is
its wing OK?"

Dr Littlewing nodded. "Yes, but that
should have made a magic seed," she
said.

Usually when a fairy did a

particularly good deed, a magic seed would appear. But a bad fairy called Lady Nightshade had cursed the Fairy Kingdom, and since then, none of the adult fairies seemed to be able to make magic seeds any more. But Poppy and her friends *had*, when they'd helped a baby otter.

Just as Poppy was thinking again about Lady Nightshade, she spotted the evil fairy's long blonde hair swishing close by. Poppy and her friends were the only ones who knew that Lady Nightshade was really their deputy head teacher, Ms Webcap! Poppy and her friends had tried to tell the teachers but they hadn't believed them.

"Ms Webcap!" Dr Littlewing called. "Come and take a look at these unusual caterpillar eggs."

Ms Webcap smiled sweetly. "Of course," she said, flying over.

Poppy frowned. She didn't trust Ms Webcap one bit. She watched as the teachers chatted about the eggs. Then Ms Webcap pointed at something in a tree. While Dr Littlewing's back was turned, Ms Webcap opened the butterfly pen – and set the butterflies free!

Chapter Two

"The butterflies!" Poppy yelled as the butterflies flew out of the pen in a rush of all different colours. "They haven't all had their medicine yet!" The fairies scattered, chasing after the escaped butterflies before they reached the sanctuary doors.

"It was Ms Webcap!" Poppy told her friends. Ms Webcap gave a smug grin

and her little black
hat – which
was secretly
a spider! –
grinned at
Poppy, waving a
leg at her.

"Ignore her!" Rose said.

"We need to help the butterflies,"
Ninad added.

They surrounded one butterfly at
a time, guiding them through the
sanctuary, past the other enclosures,
and back into the large, net-covered
pen. Eventually all of the butterflies

had been rounded up. "I don't know how they could have escaped!" Dr Littlewing muttered as she secured the door shut.

As she did, the bluebell in the corner rang. "Time for lunch," she called. "You've worked very hard this morning."

Poppy joined Rose and Ninad as they flew out of the animal sanctuary and back into Oakwings Academy. The old oak tree towered above as they flew into the Great Hall. It was bustling with noise as hundreds of fairies sat along long rows of wooden tables.

Poppy and her friends found an empty table, and Ninad's eyes widened at the piles of delicious food.

Poppy was reaching for a sunflower seed muffin when she noticed Madame Brightglow, Oakwings' head teacher, coming into the hall. She was a sunshine fairy and whenever she entered a room, it seemed to glow with a sunshiny warmth that always made Poppy feel safe and happy.

The head teacher raised her wand, sending a rainbow of colour across the Great Hall. The room immediately went quiet as all the fairies watched the rainbow. It hung in the air before fading into tiny sparkles which fluttered to the floor.

"Good afternoon, young fairies," Madame Brightglow said. "I have wonderful news. The cherry blossom is finally out!"

An excited buzz filled the hall. Poppy grabbed Rose's arm and squealed.

"You know what this means?"

"It's time for the Blossom Fair!" Rose finished.

The two girls squealed again with excitement.

"And we'll get to help organise it this year," Poppy added.

Poppy and her family had visited the Blossom Fair every year. It was one of Poppy's favourite events, and this time she would get to actually be a part of it!

"I already know what we'll have to do," Celeste boasted at the next table. "My sister told me *all* about it, so I'm

practically an expert. Did I tell you she's head fairy this year?"

Poppy glanced over at Celeste's older sister Selena. She looked just like Celeste, with the same curly brown hair, brown eyes and silver wings. She was also a teacher's pet like Celeste – she hung on to Madame Brightglow's every word as the head teacher talked to the older fairies about their duties.

Madame Brightglow held up her wand again and the room fell silent.

"For those of you who are new at Oakwings, the Blossom Fair is one of the main events in our fairy calendar.

Creatures from all over Fairy Kingdom are invited to come along and share their wonderful foods. It is a lot of fun, but also an important day. It is our job to gather the food and share it among the animals and creatures of the forest. The animals store the food to feed their families during the long, cold winter months, and we get lots of magic seeds for helping the animals!"

"Isn't it wonderful!" Ninad said with a grin. He loved doing anything he could to help the animals.

"I can't wait to try all of the amazing food," Poppy said.

"The arctic foxes in the Magic Mountains make the best ice cream," Rose said, licking her lips. "I hope they bring some!"

"I hope my aunties make their special Dewberry juice. It's the most delicious thing you will ever taste!" Ninad said.

Poppy felt a shiver of excitement run through her. She couldn't wait to get started on the preparations.

Madame Brightglow flicked her wand and towering piles of invitations appeared on each table. "Your first job is to travel across Fairy Kingdom to hand out the invitations," she told them.

Poppy glanced at some of the place names written in curly writing on the invitations.

There was Sunshine Beach, Honeysweet Hollow, the Crystal Lake and Cloudberry Caves.

"There are so many places I've never been to," she said, imagining herself eating blueberry sorbet at Sunshine Beach or swimming in the clear blue water at Crystal Lake.

She was about to ask who would go where when she noticed Ms Webcap frowning at the back of the Great Hall. While all of the other fairies were excited about the Blossom Fair, Ms Webcap seemed very unhappy.

Poppy's joy disappeared. She had a

very bad feeling deep in her tummy that Ms Webcap wasn't going to help make Blossom Fair a success. In fact, it seemed more likely she was planning to completely ruin it!

Chapter Three

"Right, first years, let's get you organised," Ms Mayblossom said as she flew over to Poppy's table.

She wore sparkly bangles along her arms which jingled when she moved. Today, her long red hair was twisted up into a bun and secured with a daisy chain. Her dress was made from bright yellow sunflower petals.

"Hi, Aunt Lily." Poppy grinned.

Poppy's aunt winked at her with sparkling eyes. "Hello, Poppy! You are going to love being part of the Blossom Fair." Then she spread out her arms and addressed the whole table.

"I have arranged you into teams," she announced to the young fairies. "Each team will go to a different area in the Fairy Kingdom to deliver the invitations."

Poppy was pleased to see that she was in a team with Ninad and Rose. She squeezed Rose's hand. "I want to go to Sunshine Beach," she said. "I've never

been there before."

Rose shook her head. "Me neither."

Ms Mayblossom pointed to the pile of invitations. "You may choose where you go," she told them. "But just to make it a bit more fun . . ."

She swished her wand and the invitations swirled into the air. "Go!"

There was a blur of wings as the fairies scrambled to first find, then grab the invitations to the place they wanted to go to the most.

"I'll get Sunshine Beach!" Rose yelled. She flew right into the middle of the invitation tornado, but one of the invitations hit her in the face, so she couldn't see where she was going. She tumbled to the ground and landed in a heap, tangled up in her wings.

"Rose!" Poppy shouted.

Rose jumped up and pulled the invitation off her face. "I'm OK!" she called, before she zipped back into the crowd.

Poppy scanned the place names written on the invitations as they twirled around. "Where is it?" she asked Ninad.

Ninad groaned. "I don't know," he said, watching the invitations whirl.

"They're making me feel a bit dizzy."

Suddenly, Poppy saw what she'd been looking for: *Sunshine Beach*. She launched forward, but Celeste appeared from nowhere and snatched the invitation up. Then she flicked her hair behind her shoulder and gave Poppy a smug look before flying back to her team.

"That was so much fun!" Rose said, landing beside Poppy and brushing her hair out of her eyes. "Sorry I couldn't get Sunshine Beach, Poppy."

"We can visit Sunshine Beach another time," Ninad said, patting

Poppy on the shoulder.

Poppy sighed. "You're right. There
are loads of other great places to visit.
Where are we going, Rose?"

Rose held up the invitation.

"Apple Tree Wood," Poppy read, then
groaned. "But that's where I'm from.
That's not an adventure at all!"

Rose looked down at the floor.
"Sorry."

Poppy squeezed her hand. "It's OK,"
she said.

Ms Mayblossom flew over to Poppy's
team.

"Oh," she said when she saw Poppy's

sad face. "At least you'll be able to see your mum and dad and give baby Daisy a hug."

Poppy brightened at the thought of seeing her family again. She had missed them so much, especially her little sister.

"I can't wait to see where you live, Poppy," Ninad said.

Rose put her arm around Poppy's shoulder. "It's going to be so much fun!"

Poppy cheered up as she grinned at her friends.

The first years gathered around Ms Mayblossom.

"You are going to need a spell to

deliver your invitations," she told them. "Hold up your wand to the invitation, tap it twice and say '*celebrato*'!"

There was a loud pop. A shower of confetti and glitter rained down on to a first-year fairy.

"Don't do it in here, Douglas!" Ms Mayblossom said, shaking her head. "Wait until you are with the people you need to invite."

She pulled out a map, and one by one began sending the teams to their destinations. "I have given each team their own magical map for this trip only," she told them. "When you have delivered your invitations, just tap your wand on Oakwings to return."

When it was Poppy's turn, Ms Mayblossom pointed her wand at Apple Tree Wood on the map. The air around them shimmered. Tiny lights appeared, spinning around and around them until they were no longer at school.

When everything stopped spinning, Poppy looked around. She saw the pretty pink and purple blossom-covered apple trees and her heart soared. "I'm home!"

She grabbed Rose and Ninad's hands

and pulled them along after her. She
wanted to show them everything.

"There's the tree where I learned how
to fly," she said. "And there's the bush
I landed in upside down when I fell.

Oh, and here's the little stream that we swim in in summertime, and the apples here are sweeter than anywhere else in the whole Fairy Kingdom."

Rose and Ninad laughed.

"It's wonderful," Rose said.

Poppy stopped suddenly and Rose flew into the back of her.

"What's wrong?" Ninad asked, looking around for signs of danger. "Is it Lady Nightshade?"

Poppy shook her head and pointed. "No, it's my house!"

She flew to a small blue door in the trunk of an apple tree and knocked

three times enthusiastically.

The door swung open and a fairy appeared, holding a baby on her hip.

"Mum!" Poppy shouted, hugging her mum and sister all at once in a tangle of arms and wings.

Her mum laughed. "Poppy! What a brilliant surprise!" she said, squeezing her tight.

The fairies flew inside. Poppy sat down on her favourite squashy chair, and Rose and Ninad did the same.

"These are my friends, Rose . . . and you remember Ninad from nursery?" Poppy asked.

"I do!" Poppy's mum said. "It's so nice to see you both."

Poppy's mum brought them a plateful of cakes and biscuits and acorn cups filled with apple juice.

"This is delicious," Ninad mumbled between sips.

Poppy told her mum and Daisy all about school and the spells they had learned. She thought about telling her about Ms Webcap too, but didn't want to worry her.

"Oh, I almost forgot," Poppy gasped.

She pulled out an invitation and her wand. "*Celebrato!*"

There was a pop as confetti and glitter rained down. Daisy giggled with delight and tried to catch the falling glitter. It swirled in the air, forming sparkly letters.

"*You are formally invited . . .*" the letters said, "*to the Blossom Fair.*"

Poppy's mum clapped. "We wouldn't miss it, would we, Daisy?" she said. "I'll make some of your favourite apple cinnamon cakes to bring."

Poppy hugged her mum tightly. "Thank you!"

Poppy's mum kissed her on the head.

"We'd better go," Ninad said. "We've

still got lots more invitations to deliver."

They said goodbye and headed back out into Apple Tree Wood, visiting every animal and fairy. They flew high up in the trees, crawled through tunnels and down into burrows underground, making sure not to miss a single home or hollow.

Finally, they reached a rabbit burrow. Outside was a small wooden sign with *Bunny Nursery* painted across it. They flew along the tunnel until it opened up into a large den. The den was filled with tiny fluffy bunnies.

Carrot mobiles hung from the ceiling, and there were warm cosy nests in the corners, made from fur and feathers. Some of the bunnies were wearing acorn shells on their heads, pretending to be fearsome knights. Others were playing in a small sand pit.

"Hello," said a large grey bunny. "I'm Mrs Bunbun, the nursery teacher."

"We have an invitation for you,"
Poppy said, holding up her wand.

The bunnies jumped around excitedly
as the glitter fell and covered their fur.

"Oh dear," Mrs Bunbun sighed at the
mess. "I'd love to come to the fair, but
with all of these cheeky bunnies to look
after I'm not sure I will have time to
make my carrot jam."

"We'll help!" Ninad shouted suddenly,
making Rose and Poppy jump as high
as the bunnies. "We'll look after the
bunnies and Mrs Bunbun will be able
to make her jam and come to the fair.
After all, it is a fairy's job to help."

Poppy and Rose shared a grin.

"You're right, Ninad," Poppy said, rolling up her sleeves. "I guess we're bunny babysitting!"

Chapter Four

While Mrs Bunbun cooked carrots in the kitchen, Poppy, Ninad and Rose played with the baby bunnies.

"They are so cute!" Rose cooed as she bounced around with the bunnies.

"Cute but tiring," Poppy gasped.

They had tried playing a few different games with the bunnies, but their favourite thing to do was to bounce around the burrow.

Ninad laughed as a bunny hopped on to his lap, snuggling her pink nose against his face.

"That tickles!" he giggled.

Mrs Bunbun came in, wiping her paws on her flowery apron. "It's time for a nap, bunnies."

"No! No! No!" shouted the bunnies.

"We don't wanna!" pouted another.

"Hop Hop Boing!" said another.

"Yes," the others echoed. "We want to play Hop Hop Boing!"

Mrs Bunbun put her paws on her hips. "If the fairies don't mind, you can

play one game of Hop Hop Boing, but then it is nap time."

"Yay!" sang the bunnies. "We promise."

Poppy looked at Ninad and Rose. "What's Hop Hop Boing?"

"It goes like this," the tiniest bunny said. He took a few steps back. "You go hop," he hopped. "Then hop again," he took another step, then, "BOING!"

He bounced toward the wall, fast!

"Stop!" Poppy shouted, afraid he would hurt himself. But he didn't. At the last second, he jumped. His big feet bounced off the wall and he *boinged*

across the room where he spun mid-air
and *boinged* again.

Soon all of the bunnies were
bouncing back and forth over the
fairies' heads.

"That looks fun!" Rose flew towards one of the walls and tried to bounce off it. Unfortunately, she wasn't as good at bouncing as the bunnies and she crashed to the floor.

"Rose!" Poppy cried, helping her friend up. "Are you OK?"

Rose brushed herself down and grinned then she flew into the air, flying back and forth with the bunnies as they hopped.

Ninad shrugged at Poppy and joined in. Soon the three of them were zooming around the room, laughing with the bunnies.

"Time for bed!" Poppy called, chasing after the bunnies.

"No!" the bunnies shouted back.

"Please!" cried Ninad.

The bunnies giggled.

Poppy landed on the floor and Ninad and Rose landed beside her. "We need to try something else," she said.

She watched the bouncing bunnies. They didn't look like they were sleepy at all.

Then she froze as she realised something. "How many bunnies were there?" she asked Ninad.

Ninad quickly counted up the

bunnies then frowned. "I thought there were ten," he said, "but . . ."

"Oh no!" Rose cried, pointing. A small bunny wiggled his tail at them before jumping out of the door. "He's trying to escape!"

The fairies chased after the bouncing bunny, all the way along the tunnel and back out into the wood.

"Stop!" Poppy puffed.

But the bunny went on hopping, right into the arms of . . .

"Mum!" Poppy cried as her mum caught the bunny.

"Looks like you three are having fun,"

her mum laughed, stroking the bunny.

Poppy sighed. "We are helping Mrs Bunbun with the baby bunnies," she said. "But they don't seem to want to have their nap."

Poppy's mum smiled. "I know just the thing to help you."

She sang a fairy lullaby and rocked the baby bunny in her arms.

"Time to sleep, my little one.

Close your eyes now, playtime's done.

Curl up, cosy in your bed.

With fairy dreams inside your head."

Soon his eyes were drooping and he had settled into a deep sleep.

"That's amazing!" Ninad said.

Poppy took the
sleeping bunny
from her
mum and
they headed
back into the
nursery.

"Let's try the
lullaby," Rose said.

The fairies sang. The bunnies' eyes
started to droop, but a few bunnies still
refused to sleep.

Poppy had an idea. "I know, let's use
the cocoon spell," she said.

She slowly spun her wand in a circle while Rose and Ninad sang. The baby bunnies watched the end of her wand go around and around, tucking the bunnies in blankets until they started to curl up into fluffy balls in their nests.

"It worked!" Poppy whispered as the baby bunnies snored.

They flew to the kitchen, and Poppy inhaled the delicious smell of carrot jam.

"That looks so good!" Ninad said.

"It's my best jam yet. And I couldn't have done it without you," Mrs Bunbun said, thanking them.

Rose, Ninad and Poppy tapped the map and went back to Oakwings tired but happy. They had managed to invite everyone in Apple Tree Wood to the Blossom Fair.

At dinner, the fairies chatted about the places they had been.

"Sunshine Beach was *amazing*!" Celeste boasted as she caught Poppy's eye. "We ate giant blueberry and melon sorbets on the sand and then went swimming!"

"Ignore Celeste," Rose said. "We'll go there together another time."

"And we did an important job

helping Mrs Bunbun," Ninad reminded
Poppy.

Poppy nodded. "And baby bunnies
are so much more fun than a boring
beach!" she laughed.

The rest of the week flew by in a
blur of activity. The fairies were busy
with the preparations for the Blossom
Fair. Poppy and her friends had been
out in the wood collecting acorns,
making nettle soup in the kitchens and
decorating the Great Hall.

While the fairies worked, they

listened to Rose and the fairy choir as they learned the Blossom Day songs, and they collected as much food as they could for the animals.

By the end of the week, everyone was exhausted. "I can't believe the Blossom Fair is tomorrow," Poppy said as they sat down for dinner.

Ninad stuffed a cherry into his mouth before he'd even sat down, and Rose, who usually couldn't stop talking, was silent as she gobbled down a slice of gooseberry pie.

Poppy looked around the hall and frowned. "Where's Aunt Lily?"

She filled a plate with food and
headed to the greenhouse to find her
aunt. Sure enough, she found Aunt Lily
among the seedlings, singing softly as
she watered them. She jumped when
she saw Poppy.

"You scared me!" she laughed.

Poppy gave her the plate of food. "I thought you might be hungry."

Aunt Lily gave Poppy a hug. "Thank you," she said. "But I don't feel very hungry. I'm so worried, Poppy. There are fewer magic seeds each day. Usually, this greenhouse is overflowing with seeds from all of the good deeds the adult fairies do. But we just can't seem to to make them any more." She sighed. "Even Madame Brightglow is starting to think that Lady Nightshade has cursed us after all."

"It's Ms Webcap," Poppy said. "If we

can stop her from . . ."

"Ms Webcap is a kind and good fairy," Aunt Lily interrupted. "She's been helping Dr Littlewing all week in the animal sanctuary. Do you think she would do that if she was Lady Nightshade?"

Poppy frowned. It didn't sound like something Lady Nightshade or Ms Webcap would do. *Why was she so interested in the animal sanctuary?* she wondered. Whatever her plan, Poppy knew it meant trouble.

Chapter Five

"Happy Blossom Fair day!" Rose shouted. She flipped off the top of her bed and landed beside Poppy.

"I'm so excited!" Poppy leaped out of bed and grabbed Rose in a hug. They laughed and twirled around their bedroom.

"Will you two stop it!" Celeste shouted from her bed.

Rose poked her tongue out at Celeste and quickly pulled a colourful petal dress over her pink wings. Poppy pulled on her favourite leaf dungarees then took Rose's hand. "Let's go!"

The Great Hall buzzed with excited

fairies eager to start the day.

"Isn't it beautiful," Poppy said,
looking around the hall. It had been
decorated with flowers and blossom.
Some hung along the walls in garlands,
some decorated the tables and doors.

Outside, hundreds of stalls had been set up by fairies and animals from far and wide. Fairies had already begun swapping and sharing food. Red and white checkered picnic blankets had been laid out for everyone to relax and try out the new treats.

"Remember, we need to keep an eye on Ms Webcap today," Poppy whispered to Rose and Ninad as they flew among the stalls. "I'm sure she's going to try something horrible."

Rose and Ninad nodded.

"We won't let her ruin the Blossom Fair," Rose said firmly.

"Oh, hello, you three!" Mrs Bunbun said as she bumped into them. She had a wagon full of jars of carrot jam and was trying to keep an eye on the baby bunnies while she set up her stall.

"Do you need help?" offered Ninad.

"Oh, that would be wonderful. Tabitha Longears, get back here—" Mrs Bunbun hopped after the bunnies who had scampered off. The three fairies set up the carrot jam in neat rows on the stall.

"Can you help the sloths, Poppy," Aunt Lily asked as she hurried by with an armful of nuts. "They are rather slow."

Poppy nodded and they headed to the sloths' stall. The smell was delicious, full of pepper and spice.

"These are sweet potato empanadas,"

one of the sloths told Poppy and her friends.

"They look amazing," Poppy said.

"Look over there," Rose said, grabbing Poppy's hand.

She dragged her over to where a badger had set up a large wooden swing. It could fit in at least ten fairies at a time and swung high up in the air then back down again.

They climbed on board, but Ninad held back. "I'll watch from here," he said nervously.

As soon as the swing moved, Rose began to shriek. Poppy laughed as they swayed up and down, until she began to feel a little sick and dizzy. She closed her eyes until the swing came to a stop.

"That was so much fun!" Rose yelled. "What shall we do next?"

"Let's look at the stalls," Poppy suggested.

They wandered among the stalls, tasting all of the different types of food. Ninad's aunties had brought along their famous Dewberry juice. It was just as delicious as he had promised and made Poppy's tummy feel a little better. They tried some of Mrs Bunbun's carrot jam, and leaf tea from the spiky echidnas.

Ninad tried some stew from the meerkats' stall that was so hot it made his eyes water.

When they were worn out and full of food, they sat down on one of the picnic blankets for a rest.

Madame Brightglow flew out of Oakwings Academy and everyone clapped. Poppy felt a warm, happy glow as she sat with her friends. Despite her worries, the Blossom Fair had been a big success.

"Thank you, friends," Madame Brightglow said. "It is wonderful to see so many of you here at the Blossom Fair. The food you have made and shared will help to feed everyone during the long winter—" she paused as a dark cloud filled the sky.

There was a low, loud rumble of thunder and a crack of lightning.

"Is it a storm?" Ninad asked.

Poppy shook her head. "No, look."

Flying high above was the shadowy figure of Lady Nightshade. She let out

an evil cackle as glittering silver letters
appeared.

**Fairy Kingdom,
Oh, you fairies love to share.
But we won't stop till your
cupboards are bare!**

At the bottom, swirly words shone:
Lady Nightshade.

With that, she disappeared and the
sun returned to the sky. The fairies and
animals muttered to themselves. But
something else was worrying Poppy.

"What did she mean when she said *we* won't stop?" she asked.

Sudden screams filled the air. Ninad held out a shaking hand. "I think she meant them!"

All around them, swarming the ground, the trees, the stalls and the food, were hundreds of tiny spiders. They began gobbling the food, gulping it down at super speed.

Poppy stared in horror. So that was why Ms Webcap had been spending so much time in the animal sanctuary!

"They weren't strange caterpillar eggs," she gasped. "They were spiders!"

Chapter Six

Ninad held out an acorn cup, trying to scoop one of the spiders into it.

"Stay back!" Dr Littlewing yelled as she flew over the crowd. "Nobody touch them!"

Dr Littlewing pointed at the spiders' backs. They each had a small red shape that looked like an hourglass.

"They are black widow spiders,"

she continued. "And they are very poisonous."

Ninad yelped and stepped away from the spider.

Everything in sight was covered in sticky webs. The spiders had smashed all of Mrs Bunbun's jars of carrot jam and had moved on to biting into some hazelnut chocolate cakes, injecting their poison into each one. A group of them worked together. Using their webs, they pulled at the stalls, making them crash to the ground.

"They're ruining everything," Rose sniffed as tears slid down her face.

"There will be no food left for the animals."

"We have to stop them!" Poppy yelled, clenching her fists.

"But how?" Rose asked, her wings buzzing.

Madame Brightglow flew at the spiders, with the teachers beside her ready to fight them off. But before she could act, the spiders shot their webs into the air. The sticky web tangled with the fairy teachers' wings. One by one they dropped to the ground, where more spiders wrapped them up until they couldn't move.

Some of the animals and fairies fled into the forest, afraid that they would be next. Poppy shook her head as she spotted Celeste and her sister flying away to hide.

"We have to help the teachers," Poppy shouted.

They flew to the teachers. Poppy tried to untangle her aunt, while Ninad helped Dr Littlewing and Rose pulled at Madame Brightglow's web.

"It's too strong!" Poppy gasped. No matter what she did, the web was stuck tight.

"I think this is moving," Rose huffed

as she pulled at a thread hanging from Madame Brightglow. The thread snapped suddenly and Rose flew backwards, somersaulting on to the floor. "Maybe not," she sighed.

"We need to find something to cut the web," Poppy said. "We'll be back soon," she called to Aunt Lily, who gave a muffled reply.

"Where's Ms Webcap?" Ninad asked nervously. The friends looked around until they spotted her. They hid behind a fallen stall and watched. She was pretending that she was trying to untie some of the other teachers, but when

she thought no one was looking, she whispered something to the spiders and they scuttled off to attack the sloths' stall.

"She's working with the spiders," Poppy said.

There was a sudden small cry close by.

Mrs Bunbun and the baby bunnies were surrounded by spiders.

"Mrs Bunbun!" Ninad said.

"Help!" she cried.

The baby bunnies cried inside their wagon as Mrs Bunbun tried to pull them to safety. But whichever way she moved, the spiders followed. They were closing in on her and the bunnies!

"We'll help you!" Rose called.

Poppy, Rose and Ninad flew overhead as the spiders creeped closer and closer to the bunnies, horrible smiles on their faces.

"Maybe we can pull them out?" Rose said.

Poppy shook her head. "There are too many bunnies, and they are too heavy for us to carry."

"There has to be another way!" Ninad shouted.

Poppy gasped as she had an idea. "Bunnies! Remember Hop Hop Boing?" she called. "I need you to do that now. As high and fast as you can. Boing, bunnies. BOING!"

The bunnies nodded at Poppy. One by one they bounced out of the wagon, landing far away from the spiders. When they were all safe, Mrs Bunbun hopped over to join them.

"You need to find somewhere safe," Poppy told them. "This way!"

She led them through the forest to a small hole in the roots of a tree and began digging at the dirt. Rose and Ninad helped, and Mrs Bunbun and the bunnies joined in. It didn't take them long to make a tunnel.

Once the bunnies and Mrs Bunbun were safely hidden inside the tunnel,

Poppy brushed the dirt from her hands.

"Now for the spiders," she said. "Do you remember the lullaby we sang to get the bunnies to sleep?" she asked her friends.

They nodded.

"Maybe it will work on spiders?" Poppy said.

Ninad grinned. "It's worth a try!"

Poppy started singing. Rose and Ninad joined in as they flew closer and closer to the spiders. The spiders paused, looking around to see where the music was coming from. A few yawned and sat down. But the rest of them continued to cause chaos, attacking the stalls, eating the food and chasing after the scared animals with their sticky webs.

"It's not working!" Poppy said. "They're going to destroy everything!"

Chapter Seven

Poppy watched the spiders, trying to come up with a plan. Some of them were yawning and moving slower, but they were still attacking the food.

"Why isn't the lullaby working?" she asked.

Ninad frowned. "Maybe we're not loud enough?"

Rose grabbed his arm. "Ninad's right.

We need more fairies – where are the fairy choir?!"

They flew through the trees, gathering as many fairies and animals as they could. Rose found her friends in the fairy choir and told them the plan. Luckily, they already knew the lullaby Poppy asked them to sing.

They started, quietly at first, then as the spiders began yawning and their eyelids drooped, they sang louder and louder.

"Time to sleep, my little one.

Close your eyes now, playtime's done.

Curl up, cosy in your bed.

With fairy dreams inside your head."

Poppy's heart soared as one by one
the spiders dropped to the ground in a
deep sleep. Maybe they could save the
Blossom Fair after all!

But then Rose yawned beside her,
and Poppy noticed that she'd stopped
singing. Ninad was still singing but his
eyes were closed.

"Wake up!" Poppy quickly shook her
friends awake. The plan had worked
– all of the spiders were falling asleep.

But it had worked *too* well. The fairies and animals were falling asleep too! What was happening?

"Just five more minutes' sleep," Rose said, lying down on the ground. The rest of the fairy choir lay down next to her, but their song carried on, echoing through the forest.

Poppy glanced around, searching for Ms Webcap. She spotted her among the broken stalls. Her eyes glittered with fury from behind her black mask. Now that the teachers had all been tied up, she had changed back into her Lady Nightshade disguise. She wore a long

cloak made from dead leaves. Her spider hat still perched on top of her head and he looked as angry as she did. She was holding out a large tube of wood like a telescope, which was playing the lullaby.

As she watched, Lady Nightshade whispered, "Amplify!" The lullaby got even louder. Mrs Webcap was making the lullaby echo louder and louder around the school. She wanted *everyone* to fall asleep.

Poppy felt her eyes start to close and forced them open. As she stared at Lady Nightshade, she realised why the lullaby wasn't affecting her. Lady Nightshade had nutshells over her ears.

With the last bit of her strength Poppy searched the ground and found

some empty acorn cups. As soon as she put them over her ears she felt the lullaby magic fade away. She picked up some more and flew to Ninad and Rose.

"Put them over your ears," she shouted, shaking Ninad awake.

"What?" he mumbled.

Poppy put the acorn shells over his ears, and he started to wake up. It worked with Rose too. But just as her friend was stirring, Lady Nightshade flew overhead.

"Pretend you're asleep!" Poppy whispered urgently.

Lady Nightshade paused for a moment, glancing down at Poppy and her friends. But Poppy kept her eyes tightly shut, and Ninad made loud snoring noises.

As she went past, a spiderweb got tangled on her wing. Grumpily, Lady Nightshade poured water on it and it dissolved.

Poppy grinned. At least they knew how to get rid of the spiderwebs now.

Once Lady Nightshade had moved on, Poppy jumped up, pulling Ninad and Rose with her.

"We have to stop her," Poppy said.

"Before she takes over the whole Fairy Kingdom."

Rose sighed. "If only we had our own spider army," she said. "Then we could trap her like the teachers."

Poppy pulled Rose into a tight hug. "That's it!" she said. "Rose, you are so clever!"

Rose frowned, then smiled. "I am?"

"The lullaby won't not work on Lady Nightshade, but the cocoon spell might," Poppy said. She looked to Ninad. "Ninad, I need you to distract her."

Ninad swallowed hard. "M–m–me?" he said.

Poppy held his hands. "You can do it, Ninad."

He took a deep breath and flew after Lady Nightshade.

After a while, Poppy heard Ninad singing. She peeped out from behind one of the stalls. Ninad was flying to

and fro with his eyes closed, singing a
strange song.

"He's pretending to sleep-fly!" Rose
giggled.

Lady Nightshade flew over to Ninad.
She waved her hand in front of his face
a few times, but when he ignored her,
she shrugged.

It was just enough time for Poppy
and Rose to sneak up behind her
and pull out their wands. As Lady
Nightshade turned to glare at them,
the young fairies spun their wands
in a circle. While Lady Nightshade
watched, helpless, a dark black cocoon

wound around
her. It started
at her feet so
she couldn't
move, then
went up
her body. It
trapped her
wings until
only her head
peeped out
from the top.

Her toadstool wand had fallen on the
floor, and the lullaby stopped.

"Let me go!" Lady Nightshade

screamed. She struggled to get free. "Webby, help me!"

The spider on her head began chewing through the cocoon.

Across the fair, the teachers were waking up. Poppy flew over, Ninad and Rose right behind her. "Look, we've caught Lady Nightshade and she is Ms Webcap!" Poppy said to Madame Brightglow, who was rubbing her eyes.

"Water gets rid of the spiderwebs, come on!" Rose said. The friends sprinkled water on the teachers' cobweb prisons and they all dissolved away.

But when they turned to look at Lady Nightshade, she was gone.

"Oh, what happened?" came a familiar voice. Ms Webcap was back in her ordinary clothes, pretending to be waking up, rubbing her eyes and shaking her wings just like Aunt Lily next to her.

Poppy glared at her, but there was nothing she could do.

"The spiders!" Dr Littlewing said as she wriggled free from the last of the spiderwebs. With the help of some of the teachers and animals, she carefully collected the snoozy spiders. Poppy,

Rose and Ninad helped, using the bunnies' wagon to help carry the spiders back to the animal sanctuary. But as they went to get it, they noticed something shimmering inside it.

Poppy bent to get a closer look. It was speckled pink and black, and she knew exactly what it was.

"A magic seed!"

Chapter Eight

"Aunt Lily! Look!" Poppy cried, holding up the seed for everyone to see.

Aunt Lily and Madame Brightglow hurried over, their eyes wide.

"You've done it again, young Poppy," Madame Brightglow said proudly. "You've managed to make a magic seed."

Poppy shook her head. "Not just me,

Madame Brightglow, it was Rose and Ninad too. We did it together."

"It must have appeared when we saved the baby bunnies," Rose said.

"Well done!" Dr Littlewing said. "You three take the spiders to the animal sanctuary. When they wake up, I'm going to have a good talk to them about their behaviour."

"When you're done, bring the seed to me," Aunt Lily said. "You can help me plant it."

The fairies hurried to the animal sanctuary where they helped Dr Littlewing put the spiders into a secure enclosure. They also checked the caterpillar eggs to make sure there were no more spider eggs hiding there.

Then they flew to the greenhouse where they found Ms Mayblossom watering the plants.

"I'm so proud of you all!" Aunt Lily gushed. "Because of you there will be a bit more fairy dust for us

to continue our magic!"

She hugged them each in turn.

They carefully planted the new seed and watered it. A small green shoot sprouted up immediately.

"Now go back and enjoy the fair," Ms Mayblossom said.

"But . . . I thought everything was ruined?" Poppy asked.

Aunt Lily grinned. "Nothing can stop Madame Brightglow when she sets her mind to something. She organised the fairies and animals to tidy and gather together all the food they could."

Poppy didn't need to be told twice. She flew out of the greenhouse, followed by Ninad and Rose.

Although it was a bit quieter, everyone was working together, helping set the stalls up, while the choir sang an upbeat tune to keep them going.

"Of course, I helped to get rid of Lady Nightshade," Celeste was saying as they passed by. "*Some* fairies flew away to hide, but I stayed to ..." she caught sight of Rose, who was staring at her with her hands on her hips.

"What were you saying, Celeste?" Rose asked.

Celeste's cheeks glowed bright red. She humphed and flew away.

"Who wants to go on the fairy wheel?" Poppy asked.

"Me, me, me!" Rose shouted.

Before Ninad had the chance to say anything, Rose and Poppy grabbed his hands and flew over to the huge fairy wheel. It was a tall wheel which spun slowly. Coconut shells hung from it, and Poppy, Rose and Ninad climbed into one as it passed.

When the wheel reached the very top,
they looked out over the forest.

"You can see for miles from up here!"
Poppy said.

"I think I can see the top of the Magic Mountains!" Rose cried.

Ninad had his hands over his eyes. "I don't want to look," he said. "It's too high up!"

Poppy laughed gently. "How can you be scared of being up high when you can fly?" she asked.

Ninad was quiet for a moment then uncovered his eyes with a sheepish grin.

When the wheel had made a full turn, they fluttered out of their coconut shell.

A little way away, Madame Brightglow stood on her own, looking

worried with a crease in her brow.

"Where next?" Rose asked, just as Aunt Lily landed beside Poppy.

Poppy pulled her aunt away from the crowds.

"I know you don't believe me, Aunt Lily, but Ms Webcap really is Lady Nightshade," Poppy said.

Aunt Lily frowned. "But Ms Webcap was asleep next to me. I saw her wake up."

"That's just what she wants you to think," Poppy said.

"I'll keep an eye on her," Aunt Lily promised. "Now go and enjoy the fair

– and celebrate! You *did* get a magic seed after all."

Poppy smiled and she and her friends headed to the stalls, trying as many foods as they could before the fair ended.

"Don't look now, but there's someone following us . . ." Ninad said.

"I think we have some fans!" Rose laughed.

The baby bunnies had surrounded them. Wherever the fairies went, the bunnies followed, chanting, "Hop Hop Boing!"

Poppy laughed. "It looks like we're

going to be doing some more bunny sitting in the future," she said, then she turned serious. "Ms Webcap almost ruined the Blossom Fair today. We're going to have to watch her even closer than ever."

"But there's always time for some fun too," Rose added, linking her arm through Poppy's.

"Come on then," Poppy grinned. "Who wants to play Hop Hop Boing?"

"Me!" The bunnies all bounced up and down in delight.

Laughing, the fairies flew off into the fair. Ms Webcap was bound to cause more trouble, but they'd be ready for her!

The End

Join Poppy for another
forest adventure in ...

The Snowflake Charm

As the bluebell rang, Poppy Merrymoss
leaped out of bed. Her wings buzzed
with excitement and her tummy
swirled with nerves as she realised what
day it was.

"Wake up, Rose!" she called to her
best friend. There was a flutter from
the bed above. Rose hung upside down
from the top bunk and squealed. "We're
going to the Snowflake Mountains!"

As soon as Poppy saw Rose's huge grin, all of her nerves disappeared. She had been a bit scared about going on her very first school trip, but anywhere she went with her best friends Rose and Ninad was sure to be fun!

Read **The Snowflake Charm** to find out what happens next!